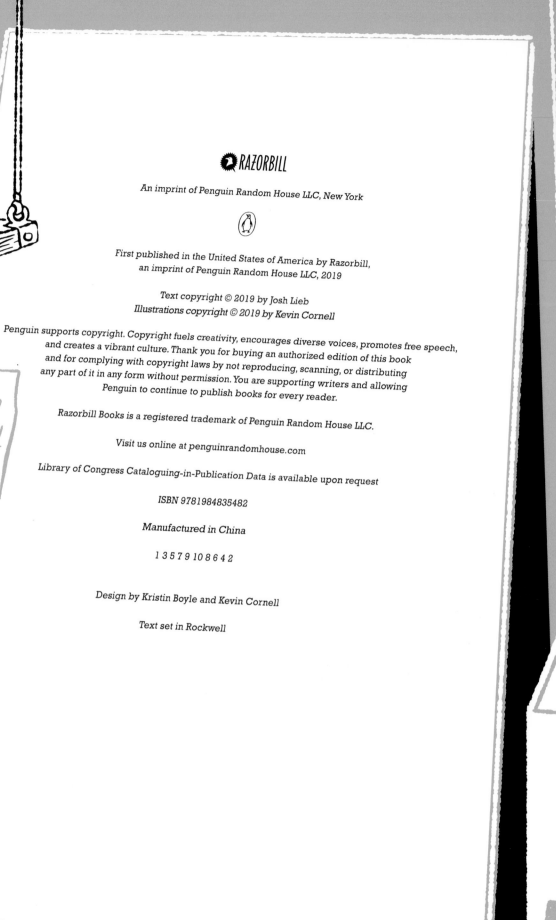

## RAZORBILL

An imprint of Penguin Random House LLC, New York

First published in the United States of America by Razorbill,
an imprint of Penguin Random House LLC, 2019

Visit us online at penguinrandomhouse.com

Library of Congress Cataloguing-in-Publication Data is available upon request

ISBN 9781984835482

Manufactured in China

1 3 5 7 9 10 8 6 4 2

Design by Kristin Boyle and Kevin Cornell

Text set in Rockwell

WET! DO
NOT
TOUCH!
– Milo

# chapter 1

**WAIT!**

I don't want to alarm you, but...

**Chapter Two is missing!**

It was definitely here yesterday, and it can't have walked off on its own, so that can only mean someone stole it.

Whoever took Chapter Two didn't leave a ransom note. I would pay any price to get Chapter Two back, obviously, because without Chapter Two the book isn't complete.

If you happen to see Chapter Two, or if you notice any suspicious characters lurking around the book, please call the police at

(925) 55 - FIND2

and ask for *Detective McGarrigan*. She's the police officer in charge of the investigation. Or you can email her at

DetMcGar@gmail.com

Or you can tweet her

@ChapterTwoBook

Now, maybe you don't believe me about Chapter Two being missing. Well, turn the page and take a look for yourself . . .

chapter

...was ...
... the

And don't ...
... you have hurt my feelings
... care about your feelings

"**And** furthermore," continued Milo the janitor, "I think you owe me an apology."

"Milo," I said, "I don't have time for apologies. Can't you see that Chapter Two is missing?!"

Milo shrugged. "That doesn't make any difference to me. I'm just the janitor here, after all."

"Then get back to work while I deal with this crisis," I said. "But first, please return the period that should be at the end of this sentence"

"I didn't think you wanted that," said Milo. "And I thought it would look better at the end of this sentence, next to the period I've already got.."

9

"Well, it doesn't look better. It looks silly," I said. "But don't bother returning it now. I don't want it after you've used it."

Milo picked up his mop and walked out, grumbling under his breath about how nobody respected a book's janitor, even though he was the one who kept the book clean enough to read.

Just then Detective McGarrigan entered.
"I have good news," she said, with a frown on her face.

"**What?**" I said. "Have you found Chapter Two?"

"No," she said.

"Well, what's the news?" I asked.

"I don't have any news," she said.

I was puzzled. "But you ended Chapter Three by telling me you had good news. Now you're telling me that you have no news?"

"Yes," said Detective McGarrigan. "And everyone knows that No News Is Good News."

I couldn't argue with that logic. After all, she's a detective.

12

"Has anybody called you at

and left a tip? Or have you gotten any emails at

Any tweets

"Yes," she said. "But I can't tell you what they said."

"Why not?" I asked.

"Because that information is supposed to be in Chapter Five."

"**But** this is Chapter Five," I said.

Detective McGarrigan looked around. "So it is," she said. "Boy, these chapters are really whizzing by. Remember when I walked in, back in Chapter Three?"

"Don't get sentimental on me," I said. "Just tell me what tips the readers have given you. Maybe one of them's a clue!"

"I don't think so," she said. "All I've gotten are messages from a bunch of crazy people telling me that I'm very, very stupid, and that you're very, very, very stupid."

"Well, that's obviously not true," I said.

"Exactly!" she agreed. "So how can I believe anything they say? Then they tell me all kinds of crazy theories—that Chapter Two is hidden on the inside back cover of the book, and that you have to use a mirror to read it, and that the thief is obviously—"

"Milo!" I yelled.

Milo came running in, dragging his mop behind him. "Now what's wrong?" he asked.

I pointed up. "What's that giant pile of *M*s doing in the middle of the page?"

"I thought you wanted those there," he said. "I think they look rather nice."

"Well, they don't look nice," I said. "They look sloppy."

"Oh," Milo said. "Do you want me to sweep them all into Chapter One? Nobody goes there anymore."

"Don't bother," I said. "I never liked Chapter Five, anyway."

"Am I still here or not?" asked Detective McGarrigan.

"You're still here," I said.

"Okay. Just checking, because I haven't said anything for a while."

She turned to Milo.

"Milo, do me a favor. Go to the end of the book and see if Chapter Two is printed on the inside back cover."

"Okay," said Milo, "But as payment, I'm going to take all the punctuation from your next three sentences."

Youd better not you scoundrel Do you have any idea who I am Ill throw you in jail you creep you weasel you animal yelled Detective McGarrigan.

"""',!?',,,!"" said Milo, and he left.

**Milo** came back. "That was fast," I said.

"A lot can happen between chapters," said Milo. "A hundred years can go by."

"Have a hundred years gone by?" I asked.

Detective McGarrigan stroked her long white beard. "I don't know."

"Did you find Chapter Two printed on the inside back cover?" I asked.

"No," said Milo, "I found something printed on the inside back cover, but it's the opposite of Chapter Two."

"What do you mean?" asked Detective McGarrigan.

Milo said, "The thing printed on the inside back cover is called owT ɿɘʇqɒʜƆ."

"Well, that doesn't make any sense," said Detective McGarrigan.

"It doesn't seem so," said Milo. "Of course, maybe it will make sense, after a little reflection." And then he laughed, as if he'd made a joke, which was very stupid of him, because of course he hadn't.

"Will you stop that infernal chuckling?" I raged. "The book is halfway over and we still haven't found Chapter Two. I need to think!"

# CHAPTER 45

"**Well,** this isn't supposed to be here," said space president Emmy Sue.

"No, it certainly is not," I said. "I don't even think it's supposed to be part of this book. This is supposed to be a mystery story, not a science fiction adventure."

"Let's just ignore it," said the space president, as she landed her rocket ship on Jupiter. "Maybe it will go away."

# chapter

**"That's** better," I said.

"What's better?" asked Detective McGarrigan.

"Don't worry about it," I said. "You weren't there. Now, where were we?"

"You just made me stop chuckling because you said you needed to think," said Milo.

"That's right," I said, "I did. And I still can't think, because you people won't stop talking. So here's what we're going to do. Everyone is going to be absolutely quiet for three whole chapters. Understand? No talking."

"Beginning when?" asked Detective McGarrigan.

"Beginning . . . NOW."

chapter

9

chapter
10

# chapter
# 11

"**I've** got it!" I said, and I snapped my fingers.

Detective McGarrigan collapsed on the floor. Her face had turned purple.

"You idiot," I said. "I said no talking—I didn't say you had to hold your breath."

Her eyes fluttered open. "I . . . misunderstood," she whispered.

After she recovered, I explained to her that I'd solved the mystery. "Only one person has been acting suspiciously and shifting things around and stealing things throughout this whole book. Therefore, the person who stole Chapter Two is obviously   ilo!"

I smiled triumphantly.

"Who's Ilo?" asked Detective McGarrigan.

"Not Ilo!" I said, " ilo!" That didn't come out right. I tried again. " ilo! ilo!" But I still couldn't say it. "I see what happened," I said. "He stole all the  s out of  y sentences so I couldn't say his na  e."

"His what?" asked Detective McGarrigan.

"Then he stashed the whole big pile of stolen  s in Chapter Five," I said. "That  an is a  enace! A  onster!

"Oh, you mean the *M*s," said Detective McGarrigan. She looked around the chapter.

"Say, where's Milo?"

"Oh  y goodness!" I said. "He's  issing!"

"**Can** we skip this chapter?" asked the detective nervously. "I'm superstitious, and thirteen is a very unlucky number."

But I was already halfway through. I'd spotted something in the next chapter. It looked like a handwritten note from Milo.

**By** "handwritten," I mean that Milo had traced his hand and written on it so that it looked like a turkey. He had labeled the turkey *You*. I don't know why he would want to insult you, though. He doesn't even know *you*. I guess he's just rude.

On the other side of the paper, he had typed a message.

33

# The message said:

You fools have turned
me into a criminal.

Now I have escaped.
And you will never
get your precious
Chapter Two back.

Love,

— Milo

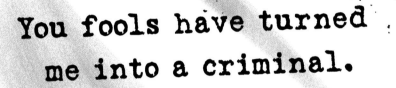

Detective McGarrigan said, "I wonder if that was written by the same Milo we know."

"It has to be our Milo," I said.

"Not necessarily," said Detective McGarrigan. "There are lots of people named Milo in the world."

"Yes," I said. "But if it was written by a Milo we didn't know, he wouldn't have signed it 'Love.'"

Detective McGarrigan was impressed. "You should be a detective," she said.

"So that's that," I said. "We've solved the case. The villain is Milo."

"But where is Chapter Two? And why did Milo steal it?" asked Detective McGarrigan.

I shrugged. It was the kind of shrug that says *There are some things we'll never know.*

Detective McGarrigan shrugged, too. It was the kind of shrug that says *A cockroach crawled down my back.* That kind of thing never happened when this book had a janitor.

Of course, if you happen to stumble across Chapter Two, or if you have any idea why Milo turned to crime, please call

(925) 55-FIND2

or tweet

@ChapterTwoBook

or email the detective at

DetMcGar@gmail.com

My personal theory is that there never was a Chapter Two, and Milo only pretended there was one in order to distract me while he stole the Hope Diamond, which I had left hidden under your bed.

Go look under your bed now. If a giant blue diamond isn't there, you'll know that Milo succeeded.

It's not there, is it? I was right!

I guess that janitor is sorry he ever tangled with a genius like me.

You may have escaped me this time, Milo. But you'll make a mistake someday.

WESTERN

HISTORICAL FICTION

HORROR

YOUNG ADULT

REVENG
FANTAS

OLD
ADULT

MYSTERY

SCIENCE FICTION

WAKUKUBE DEPARTMEN

And on that day, I will be waiting, like a cat. That is waiting for a mouse. Who stole the Hope Diamond . . .
And the mouse thinks it got away with it, but there will be a cat there. Waiting.
And that cat will be me.
And I will be waiting.
Like a cat.

"You know," Milo said, "I have half a mind to steal this chapter of the book and hide it someplace that you'll never find it. Then you'll be sorry!"

"But I'll know that you stole it," I said.

"Not if this chapter is missing!" he replied.

I rolled my eyes. "I happen to be friends with Detective McGarrigan of the police force. She'd catch you before you got to another page!"

Milo got a very serious look on his face. He put his mop over his shoulder and stared me straight in the eye: "That's it. I'm going to do it."